Spartan + FRIENDS
I0746537

Hazel and Spartan's Halloween Trail
Colouring and Literacy Book

Consolidating phonics knowledge with extended decodable text.

Word Count
Approx. 462 words

ai / ay → trail, day, way
ee / ea → steed, need, beam, dream
igh → bright, night
ar → Spartan, armour
oo → moon, soon, spooky
ch → cheer, children
sh → she, show, wish

High-Frequency Words
a, and, the, of, in, on, with, to, for, is, it, they, he, she, we,
was, said, all, your, you, I, that, this, here, near, out, not, so, by, from, at

Irregular Words
said, come, your, you, are, was, again, they, their, here

Practice Words
Spartan, dragon, princess, knight, ghost, bumblebee, lanterns, pumpkin,
armour, sword, costume, ribbon, scales, crown, fairy, pirate, witch, lollies,
candy, treats

Teacher Prep Before Reading

Review ai and ee diagraphs with word cards (trail, sweet, green).
Practice igh trigraphs (night, bright, knight).

Vocabulary support: Introduce costume, princess, knight, dragon,
ghost, lantern, pumpkin, armour, sword, fairy, witch, treats.

Miss Laura called, "Your lesson is done,
the horses are tired, but we've had fun.
Don't forget, next week's the Halloween Trail,
I can't wait to show you the fun we've planned,
I will not fail."

"Bring your costume, dress up bright,
our trick-or-treat ride will be at night.
Your parents will wait in costumes neat,
along the track with secret treats."

Hazel grinned and stroked her steed,
already dreaming of what she'd need.
She whispered, "Spartan, we'll look grand,
the finest horse in all the land."

That week at home she made her plan,
with ribbons, cloth, and glue in hand.
Hazel chose a princess gown,
a pink silk dress with a golden crown.

Spartan's costume made her beam,
a dragon horse, just like a dream.
With shiny wings and scales of blueish green,
the best dragon horse you've ever seen.

Her friends dropped by with grins so wide,
to share the plans they could not hide.
Huxley said, "Suki's a bumble bee,
with yellow stripes for all to see!"

Oliver laughed, "I'll be a knight,
and Tucker my noble steed of might.
With silver armour, bold and bright,
and a shining sword held good and tight."

Sophie said, "Dot will be a ghost in white,
she'll glow and shimmer through the night."
They all buzzed loud with fun and cheer,
the ride was close, it soon was here!

The moon rose high, the stars did glow,
The lanterns lit in a golden row.
Miss Laura smiled, "Come gather near,
your Halloween ride is finally here!

Here are your maps, all marked with care,
find pumpkins to see where treats are near.
Each pumpkin shows a place to meet,
where parents wait with tasty treats."

"Ride safe and kind, stay with your crew,
the trail is set and marked for you.
Enjoy the fun, now off you go!"
She waved them on and watched the show.

Clip-clop, clip-clop, the riders went,
each horse in costume, riders content.
First stop was a pirate dad with gold,
next a witch with lollies to hold.

A fairy waved with sparkling cheer,
"Happy Halloween! take treats here!"
A pumpkin mum with a glowing face,
handed out cakes wrapped up in lace.

They laughed and rode from spot to spot,
their bags grew full, they ate a lot.
They followed their maps and found each place,
with happy smiles on every face.

Spartan pranced, his wings held high,
a dragon horse beneath the sky.
Hazel laughed, her crown did gleam,
her princess ride was like a dream.

Back at the barn the children said,
with candy shared and horses fed:
"This was such an amazing day,
in every single, spooky way.
With friends and sweets and Halloween cheer,
we hope Miss Laura does this again every year!"

Activities (for after reading)

1. Re-read the story and circle words with igh pattern (night, bright)

2. Find and <u>underline</u> all the words with ee (steed, sweet)

3. Write 3 new sentences with or words (sword)

____

____

____

____

____

____

____

4. What was your favourite costume? _________________________

5. Fill the gap: "They all ___________ loud with fun and cheer."

Activities (for after reading)

6.Can you write a new verse about another rider and the costume they might choose?

____

____

____

____

____

____

____

____

____

____

Activities (for after reading)

7. Write some words that rhyme with, dream.

____

____

8. Can you name three things the kids used to dress up the horses?

____

____

____

9. What was the most fun part for the children, creating the costumes, following the map, receiving the treats, Why?

____

____

____

____

____

Activities (for after reading)

10. Can you retell the important parts of the story?

____

____

11. What was your favourite part of the story?

____

____

____

12. Imagine the Trail map, what do you think it looked like?
Draw a picute of what you image below:

Activities (for after reading)

13. Find all the rhyming words in the story and write them below.
For example night – bright – knight – might.
Then add your own to rhyme with those words.

____

____

____

____

14. Complete the words with the missing sounds:

Sp__tan

kn___t

tr__l

gr__n

h__se

15. Colour in all of the story pages.

Spartan + Friends